Dear Parent:
Your child's love of reading starts here!

Every child learns to read in a different way and at his or her own speed. Some go back and forth between reading levels and read favorite books again and again. Others read through each level in order. You can help your young reader improve and become more confident by encouraging his or her own interests and abilities. From books your child reads with you to the first books he or she reads alone, there are I Can Read Books for every stage of reading:

SHARED READING
Basic language, word repetition, and whimsical illustrations, ideal for sharing with your emergent reader

BEGINNING READING
Short sentences, familiar words, and simple concepts for children eager to read on their own

READING WITH HELP
Engaging stories, longer sentences, and language play for developing readers

READING ALONE
Complex plots, challenging vocabulary, and high-interest topics for the independent reader

ADVANCED READING
Short paragraphs, chapters, and exciting themes for the perfect bridge to chapter books

I Can Read Books have introduced children to the joy of reading since 1957. Featuring award-winning authors and illustrators and a fabulous cast of beloved characters, I Can Read Books set the standard for beginning readers.

A lifetime of discovery begins with the magical words "I Can Read!"

Visit www.icanread.com for information
on enriching your child's reading experience.

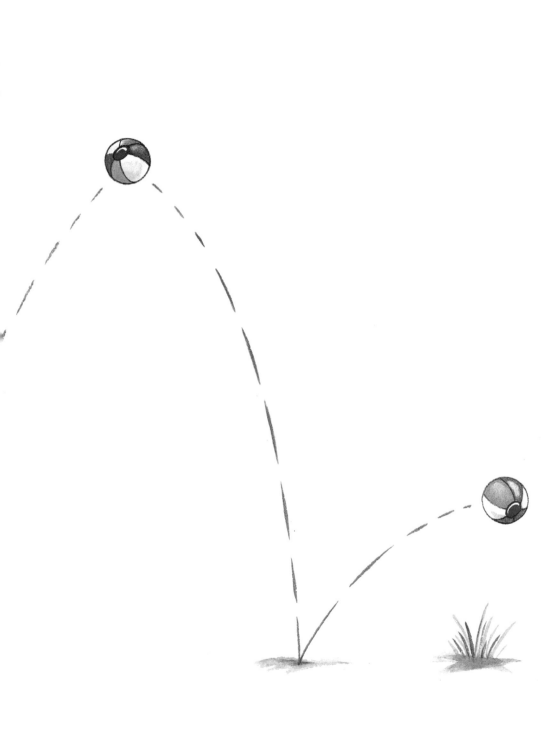

Biscuit's New Trick

story by ALYSSA SATIN CAPUCILLI
pictures by PAT SCHORIES

HarperCollins*Publishers*

Biscuit's New Trick Text copyright © 2000 by Alyssa Satin Capucilli Illustrations copyright © 2000 by Pat Schories All rights reserved. No part of this book may be used or reproduced in any manner whatsoever without written permission except in the case of brief quotations embodied in critical articles and reviews. Printed in the United States of America. For information address HarperCollins Children's Books, a division of HarperCollins Publishers, 10 East 53rd Street, New York, NY 10022.
www.harpercollinschildrens.com

Library of Congress Cataloging-in-Publication Data

Capucilli, Alyssa.
   Biscuit's new trick / story by Alyssa Satin Capucilli ; pictures by Pat Schories.
      p.   cm.—(A my first I can read book)
   Summary: A puppy does all sorts of tricks in the process of learning the one his master is trying to teach him.
   ISBN-10: 0-06-028067-0 (trade bdg.) — ISBN-13: 978-0-06-028067-3 (trade bdg.)
   ISBN-10: 0-06-028068-9 (lib. bdg.) — ISBN-13: 978-0-06-028068-0 (lib. bdg.)
   ISBN-10: 0-06-444308-6 (pbk.) — ISBN-13: 978-0-06-444308-1 (pbk.)
   [1. Dogs—Training—Fiction.] I. Schories, Pat, ill. II. Title. III. Series.
Pz7.C179Biu 2000   99-23004
[E]—dc21   CIP
                                                                                                          AC

❖

13 14 15 16 17 LP/WOR 40 39 38 37 36 35 34

For Anthony and Ruby, the newest
—A.S.C.

To Laura
—P.S.

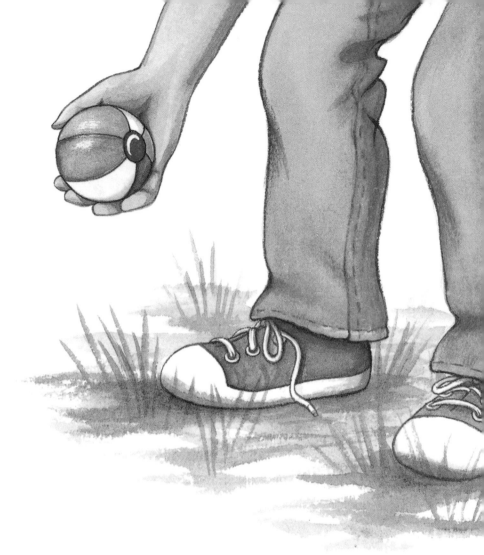

Here, Biscuit!
Look what I have.
Woof, woof!

It's time to learn
a new trick, Biscuit.
Woof, woof!

It's time to learn
to fetch the ball.
Ready?

Fetch the ball, Biscuit.

Woof, woof!

Silly puppy!

Don't roll over now.

Get the ball, Biscuit.

Fetch the ball, Biscuit.

Woof, woof!

Where are you going,
Biscuit?
Woof!

Funny puppy!
Fetch the ball,
not your bone.

Let's try again.

Fetch the ball, Biscuit!

Woof, woof!

Good puppy!
You got the ball.
Woof!

Wait, Biscuit.

Bring the ball back!

Woof, woof!

17

Let's try one more time.

Fetch the ball, Biscuit!

Woof, woof!

Oh no!
Not in the mud!

Stop, Biscuit!
Don't fetch it now!
Woof!

Oh, Biscuit!

You did it!

You learned a new trick!

Woof, woof!

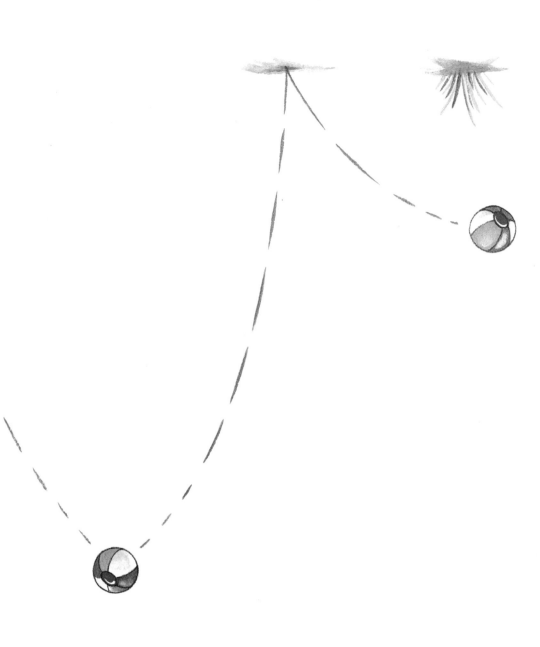